MR. CHATTERBOX

by Roger Hargreaves

EGMONT

Mr Chatterbox was one of those people who simply couldn't stop talking.

He used to talk to anybody and everybody about anything and everything, going on and on and on.

And on and on and on!

And on and on and on!

And, when he didn't have anybody else to talk to, he used to talk to himself.

"Good morning, Mr Chatterbox," he used to say to himself.

"Good morning to you," he used to reply to himself.

"Nice day, isn't it?"

"Yes, it is, for the time of year."

And so on, and so on, and on and on!

He lived in a box-shaped house in a village.

Chatterbox Cottage!

One morning, the postman arrived with a letter for him.

"Morning, Mr Chatterbox," said the postman.

"Ah, good morning to you, Postman," replied Mr Chatterbox. "Although, as I was saying to myself only yesterday, or was it the day before, I forget, however, it's not quite so good a morning, in my opinion, but I might be wrong, although I'm not very often, as it was the other day, Monday I think it was, or perhaps it was Tuesday, but never mind, because it is quite a good morning, don't you agree, yes of course you do, because that's what you said to me in the first place, and …"

And he went on and on, all morning, and the poor postman was late delivering all his letters.

That afternoon, Mr Chatterbox went into the hat shop in the village.

"Hello, Mr Bowler," he said to the man who owned the hat shop. "Do you think, if it's possible, that I could buy, if it's not too expensive, but I'm sure it won't be, a new hat, because, would you believe it, yes of course you would, but anyway, as I was saying, my present hat, the one on my head, as you can see, is getting, how can I put it, a little too old, because I've had it for, let me see now, it must be, let's think, ten years, no, I tell a lie, it can't be that long, or can it, well yes it could be, but on the other hand …"

And he went on and on all afternoon and half the night, long after poor Mr Bowler should have shut up shop and gone home.

Eventually, when Mr Bowler managed to get a word in edgeways (or was it sideways), he promised to order a new hat for Mr Chatterbox.

Then he pushed Mr Chatterbox out of his shop, still talking of course, and went home for his supper, which was cold of course, because Mrs Bowler had cooked it for him hours ago.

And, while he ate, he thought.

Exactly one week later the new hat for Mr Chatterbox arrived, in a smart red hatbox.

The postman delivered it to Mr Bowler's shop.

"At last," said Mr Bowler, heaving a sigh of relief. "I think this hat is going to be the answer to the problem of Mr Chatterbox talking so much."

"I wish it could be," said the postman. "But how can it?"

"Because," replied Mr Bowler, "this hat is a magic hat!"

"Oh," replied the postman, who didn't quite understand.

That same afternoon, Mr Bowler took the new hat round to Chatterbox Cottage.

"Oh goody," said Mr Chatterbox, seizing the hatbox and opening it. "It's my new hat, my lovely new hat, I couldn't wait for it to arrive, in fact, I got up early this morning, because, aren't I silly, I just knew, I don't know how, but I really knew, you know, that today would be the day, I don't know how I knew, but I knew, and it is, and here's my hat, and oh, isn't it beautiful, I can't wait to try it on, oh I do hope it suits me, do you think it will, yes of course you do, and …"

"Why don't you try it on?" said Mr Bowler, grinning.

"Try it on? Yes, of course I must try it on, how silly of me to stand here chattering on when I haven't tried it on yet, yes, I will, absolutely, definitely, try it on straight away, because, as I said, it's silly just to talk about trying it on, and then not try it on, isn't it, and so …"

He took the hat out of the hatbox, and put it on.

It was a beautiful hat!

"I say," he said. "I must say, yes I really must, that this hat is, yes it really is, to say the least, one of the better hats that I have ever seen in my life, and in this life, I must say, I have seen some hats, and furthermore …"

But, while he was talking, a funny thing was happening.

The more words that came out of Mr Chatterbox's mouth, the larger his hat became.

The more Mr Chatterbox talked, the more the hat grew, and grew.

Mr Chatterbox kept on talking, and the hat kept on growing.

"I can't see anything," he said. "One minute I was standing here admiring my new hat, and now, all of a sudden, without any warning, taking me all unawares, just like that …"

The hat grew down to his feet, and Mr Chatterbox stopped talking.

And, as soon as he stopped talking, the hat grew smaller and smaller, until it was the same size as when he'd first tried it on.

Mr Bowler had gone when Mr Chatterbox couldn't see him.

And now he was walking back to his shop.

"My special magic hat really works," he chuckled.

The following day, Mr Chatterbox was out for a walk when he met the postman in the village.

"Hello, Postman," he said. "I say, do you like my new hat, have you ever seen such a fine hat, I'm sure you never have, what a hat, and …"

But you know what was happening, don't you?

The hat grew and grew and grew the more
Mr Chatterbox talked.

"Now I know what Mr Bowler meant by a magic hat,"
chuckled the postman.

And he went on his way, leaving poor Mr Chatterbox
speechless.

"Hmm," he thought, thinking. Not talking – thinking!

And do you know something?

That hat taught Mr Chatterbox his lesson.

And these days he doesn't talk half as much as he used to, or even a quarter as much. And you know the reason for that, don't you?

Yes, of course you do.

But …

… keep it under your hat!